Make Way for Water

by ELEANOR CLYMER

Illustrated by J. C. WONSETLER

jC629ma

JULIAN MESSNER, INC.   NEW YORK

Published by Julian Messner, Inc.
8 West 40th Street, New York 18
Published Simultaneously in Canada
by The Copp Clark Co., Ltd.
Copyright 1953, by Julian Messner, Inc.
Printed in the United States of America

Library of Congress Catalog Card No. 53–10499

Make Way for Water

Peter Venner came out on the back porch of his father's house and looked up at the hills. The white farmhouse was at the foot of the valley, and the blue hills stood around it like a high, dark wall. It was early in the morning. The sun had not yet come up over the edge of the wall. There was some mist on the hills, but Peter knew it would clear off later. It was going to be another hot day. Peter could always tell by looking at the hills what the weather was going to be like.

He took a bite of the doughnut he held in his hand, and started to climb the hill behind the house.

Peter was eleven, and he helped his father take care of the cows and the gardens. He had his own calf that he had raised from the time it was born.

This morning, when the cows came down from the upper pasture, the calf had not come with them. Peter would have to go and find it. He trudged up the hill, calling as he went.

"Soo-key! Soo-key!"

The pasture was dry. It had been a dry summer, though Peter's father wasn't too worried. There was plenty of water on the farm for the gardens and the cattle. There was the creek flowing down through the middle of the valley. There was a good well on the farm, and there were springs on the hillsides that never went dry. It was true that the grass was brown and burned from lack of rain. Probably that was why the calf was lost. It had wandered off to look for better grazing.

But the people in the city needed water. There was a great shortage. Father read about it in the paper every day, and when Peter wasn't too busy to pay attention he heard him talking about it. The city's reservoirs were only half full, and the people would have to build some new ones. The ones they had didn't hold enough water to last over a dry season like this.

Peter hadn't thought much about the city people. He didn't see what he could do, and anyhow he was too busy with his own affairs to worry about them.

Higher and higher he went, until he could look down on the roof of the white house and on the barns and gardens. He loved the farm. He liked to look down on it and think, All that is ours! Now he could see the cows coming out of the barn. They had been milked, and they stopped at the trough in the barnyard to drink and then ambled on into the pasture.

Peter climbed on. There was a patch of woods up ahead. Maybe his calf was in there.

He pushed aside a low branch and plunged in.

"Soo-key!" he called. Then he stood still to listen.

He heard something crashing around in the brush, but it didn't sound like a calf. It sounded like people. Then he heard voices, a man's and a boy's.

He called out, "Hello! Who's there?"

"Hi!' said the man's voice. And the boy called, "Who are you?"

Peter was puzzled. Who was this asking, "Who are you?" on his father's land? He went

8

on till he saw them, a tall man in a checked shirt and sun hat with a map in one hand, and a redheaded boy about his own age.

What were they doing there with a map?

"My name's Peter Venner," said Peter. "I'm looking for my calf. Have you seen a brown calf around here?"

"Yes, we saw one," said the man. "She's grazing on the other side of these woods. My name's Carter, and this is my son Mike. We came up the hill from the other side. I suppose

we're on your father's land. We'll go down this way and speak to him."

Peter nodded. He supposed Dad wouldn't mind, but what were they doing with the map? And the man had a compass in his hand. Peter couldn't figure it out.

"You visiting around here?" he asked. He was used to summer visitors.

"Well, not exactly," said the man. "We're from the city."

"My dad's from the Water Supply Department," the boy broke in. "There's going to be a new reservoir here. I bet you didn't know." He grinned cheerfully.

Peter stared at him. What was the boy talking about? A new reservoir here! That sounded pretty silly. Then he saw that the man was looking at his son with disapproval.

"Mike," he said, "I thought you knew better than to speak out like that. If you can't be more careful, I'll just have to leave you home."

"What do you mean, mister?" Peter asked. "Is he telling the truth?"

"Well," said the man, "I don't know for sure. It wouldn't be fair to tell you yes or no. That's one of the things I have to speak to your father about."

Peter looked up at the man. He seemed like a nice person. But that wasn't what mattered.

"Mister," he said, "I can tell you one thing, there's not going to be any reservoir here. My dad wouldn't have it."

He turned away and crashed through the brush. As he came out into the sunlight he saw the brown calf.

"Moo!" it said, and ran toward him to rub its head against his sleeve. He led it down the hill to the barn. As he went, he thought about what the boy had said. It sounded like a lot of nonsense. But he couldn't help feeling scared. What if it were true?

He wanted to tell his father about it right away, but Father had driven off somewhere. So Peter stayed at the barn. By the time he got through brushing burrs out of the calf's coat it was nearly lunchtime. He went up to the house.

There was a green car parked in the driveway. Peter went indoors. There in the kitchen, sitting at the table with his mother and father, was that man!

"Hello, there," said the man.

"Hello," said Peter.

"Oh," said Father, "do you two know each other?"

"We met on the hill," said Mr. Carter. "Well, I must be going. I'll see you again. Good-by."

As soon as he was gone, Peter burst out, "What did he want?"

13

"He wants to buy our farm," said Father.

"Buy our farm!" Peter exclaimed. "What for?"

"There's going to be a new reservoir," said Father. "They're going to buy all the farms in this valley and build a dam and flood the whole valley."

"But you aren't going to sell *our* farm!" Peter cried.

"Well, I guess I'll have to," said Father. "They're offering a very good price."

"But Dad!" Peter protested, looking from his father to his mother. "You don't seem to *care!*" He didn't see how they could sit there so calmly.

"Well, I'm not surprised," said Father. "I've seen it coming. It's been in the papers for weeks. I've been telling you about it."

So that was what he had been talking about!

"We'll get another farm," said Mother. "We're sorry to leave this one, but Father knows of a very good farm he can buy. I think you'll like it when you see it."

"I won't!" Peter shouted angrily. "I'll never

14

go anywhere else. I'll never like any other farm." And he stamped out of the room. He had never been so angry or so unhappy in his life.

His father came after him. "Mr. Carter's going to speak to all the farmers at the meetinghouse tonight," he said. "Maybe you'd better come along. Then you'll understand why the city people need a new reservoir."

"I don't care about those city people," Peter muttered.

But when evening came he put on the clean shirt his mother gave him, and went along.

Mr. Carter was there on the platform. He had a big map stuck up on the wall and he was explaining it to the people.

"This is a map of the whole region," he said. "You see, this is your valley. It makes a very good watershed."

Then he showed them what a watershed was, how the rain and spring water ran down the hillsides to the river at the bottom. He drew pictures to show how the water would get to the city through huge aqueducts; how it would run

15

KEY.
AREA OF WATERSHED
RESERVOIR
VIADUCT
VIADUCT
RIVER
RIVER
CITY
BAY

downhill by its own weight all the way, because the city was at sea level while the reservoirs were up in the hills.

"There's a river runs right past the city," said somebody in the audience. "Why can't they use that? Why can't they dig wells the way we do?"

"The river is a tidal river," said Mr. Carter. "The water is too salty to use, except for putting out fires. Wells wouldn't give nearly enough water. Some cities have wells and pumping stations, but ours is too big."

"But the city has a lot of reservoirs," said somebody else. "Why does it need more?"

"The city is growing all the time," Mr. Carter answered. "A few years ago there were five million people and they were using about a hundred gallons of water apiece every day. Now there are more than eight million, and they use a hundred and fifty. That's more than a billion gallons a day."

There were whistles and exclamations. "Shouldn't take so many baths," said somebody in the front row.

Mr. Carter laughed. "It isn't all baths," he said. "It's water for washing streets and fighting fires. There are cooling systems and laundries and ice plants and bottling plants. And don't forget the factories. They use terrific amounts of water, and every year they need more. We've got to plan a water system that will last for years."

Peter sat there and listened. He watched Mr. Carter draw diagrams on the blackboard. He saw that there were other reservoirs up in the hills, and it made sense to build a new one not too far from them, so the same aqueducts could be used.

But he could really think of only one thing. His valley was going to be dammed up to make a lake. His farm was going to be flooded. He would never again walk out on the porch and look up at the hills and wait for the sun to come up over them. The more he thought about it the worse he felt. He was glad it was dark when he walked home with his parents so they couldn't see his face.

Weeks went by. Father was very busy. He was driving around, looking at farms, talking to the neighbors. He asked Peter to go with him, but Peter wouldn't. He stayed home and took care of his calf and his garden.

Then one day Mr. Carter came back. He got out of the car to talk to Mr. Venner and Mike jumped out, too. He started toward Peter, but Peter gave him a chilly look.

"Huh!" he said to himself. "One of those city kids that needs so much water."

The grownups were all going to drive up the valley to make arrangements about moving the schoolhouse. But Peter didn't want to go.

"All right, then," said Mother, "Mike can stay here and keep you company."

This was even worse. Peter wished Mike would go away and leave him alone. But Mike wouldn't do that. He followed him all over the farm. He was full of admiration for everything.

"Golly! Is that your garden? Did you plant it yourself? Is that your calf? What are you going to do with her? Sell her? Oh, boy, look at the kittens!"

Peter tried to think of something to do that Mike wouldn't like. He decided to clean out the calf shed. He turned on the hose and began to wash the floor. But Mike thought it was fun. He grabbed a shovel and started to help, pushing the stream of mud and dirt out through the door. Peter couldn't help thinking Mike was a pretty good sport after all.

Mike was interested in everything. "Does the water come from the creek?" he asked.

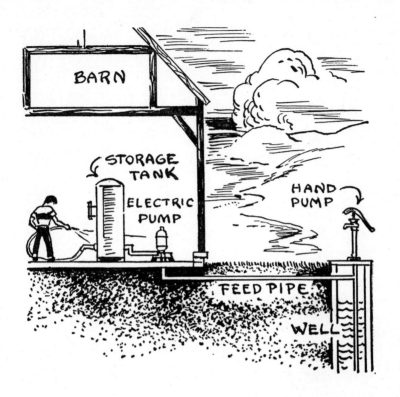

BARN

STORAGE TANK

ELECTRIC PUMP

HAND PUMP

FEED PIPE

WELL

"No," said Peter. "It's from the well."

"How does it get to the hose?" Mike persisted. "Where do you get your pressure?"

"There's a pump in the barn," said Peter. He showed Mike the electric pump that forced water into a tank.

"Oh, I see," said Mike. He looked around at

the barn. "This is a swell place," he said. "It's a shame you have to move. I don't blame you for being mad."

That gave Peter an idea. Maybe he could get Mike on his side. "Well, why don't you tell your father to pick some other place for the reservoir?" he asked.

Mike shook his head. "It wouldn't do any good," he said unhappily. "I—I asked him already."

"You did?" said Peter.

"Uh-huh. But he hasn't got anything to do with the plans. It wasn't his idea. There's a whole department in the city, and they decide. It's just Dad's job to come here and talk to the people. He doesn't like it, either."

Peter could see that, of course. In a way it made him feel worse, because it meant there was nothing he could do about it. But in another way he felt better because he really liked Mr. Carter and Mike. Mike was a good kid.

"Come on," he said, "let's go down to the creek for a swim."

Before they could get started, the grownups came back. Mr. Carter was in a hurry. He had to start for the city at once.

"Oh, shucks," said Mike. "We were just going swimming."

"Well, you'll have to go some other time," his father said.

Suddenly Mike grinned. "I have an idea, Pop," he said, "let's take Peter with us."

Mr. Carter looked surprised. "Take Peter with us?" he repeated. "Well——" And then the idea seemed to appeal to him. "Sure, why not?" he said. "That is, if Peter wants to come. I think it's a fine idea. What about it, Peter?"

Peter didn't know what to say. He had never been to the city. And though he liked Mike better now than he had at first, he was still one of those city kids. He looked at his father and mother.

"It might be a very good idea," his mother said slowly. "That is, if Mike's mother won't mind."

"Oh, she likes company," said Mike. "Come on; get ready."

In almost no time Mother had packed a lunch and put Peter's things in a suitcase, and they were on their way.

PART II

Mike and Peter sat in the back of the car while Mr. Carter drove. They had fun. Now that Peter was away from the farm he could stop thinking about it for a while. They played alphabet games, looking out at the signs along the way. They counted white cows and black horses, and they laughed a lot about nothing much. They ate the lunch Mrs. Venner had packed. Every little while Mike would say, "I'm thirsty." Then his father would stop and buy them soda or ice cream. It was very hot. The sun beat down on the car.

"We'll come to a shady stretch pretty soon," said Mr. Carter. And sure enough, in a little while they saw wide-spreading pine trees on both sides of the road. On the left a hillside sloped down to a lake. Peter could see the blue water between the black treetrunks. The cool smell of pine needles filled the air.

"I'd like a swim in that lake," said Peter.

"You can't swim in it," said Mr. Carter, "because it isn't a lake. It's one of our reservoirs."

So this was a reservoir! Peter hadn't imagined it would be so big. They drove along the edge of it for miles, and most of the way the water was screened from the dust of the road by trees.

25

They saw a motorboat going back and forth in a zigzag course.

"What's the matter with those people?" Peter asked. "Don't they know where they're going?"

Mr. Carter laughed. "They aren't going anywhere," he said. "They're dragging sacks full of chemicals through the water to purify it." He stopped the car at the entrance to a broad

stone highway that went straight across the water. He climbed out and started walking across it. The boys followed him.

"Are we going to walk across this bridge?" Peter asked.

"It's not a bridge," said Mr. Carter. "This is the dam."

"Golly!" Peter breathed.

On one side was the lake, a wide sheet of blue water dotted with islands. On the other side they looked down, down, down along a high stone wall to the ground far below. It was enormous. Peter could hardly believe that ordinary people had been able to build a wall strong enough to hold back all that water—thirty billion gallons, Mr. Carter had said! And somewhere, not far away, buried in the earth, was the aqueduct, the big pipe that took the water to the city. It was a huge tunnel eighteen feet high with walls of concrete and steel.

Peter could have stood there staring for a long time, but Mr. Carter hurried them back to the car. He drove across the dam and then back along the reservoir about a mile till they came to a small stone building.

"This is a gatehouse," he said. "Here is where the water flows out of the reservoir into the aqueduct."

He knocked at the door and a man came out.

"Hello, Mr. Callahan," said Mr. Carter.

"Why, hello!" said Mr. Callahan. "I haven't seen you in a long time! And have you got two boys now?"

"No," said Mr. Carter. "This one is Peter Venner. He's a friend of ours. We're showing him the reservoir."

"Ah, it's low now," said Mr. Callahan, shaking his head. "If we don't get some rain, I don't know what we'll do. Look!" He leaned over the railing and pointed down into the water. Peter peered over the edge. "It's so low," the man said, "you can see where a village used to be."

Sure enough, through the blue water Peter could faintly see the outline of a road. He thought he could even see where the foundations of a house had once stood.

"Well, come on in," Mr. Callahan was saying. Peter followed him into the gatehouse. They were in a room full of strange machines. There were controls to open and close the gates far down in the pipes, and gauges to show how much water was going through. There was a ladder that went down through the floor to the pipes, so that men could go down and make repairs.

Mr. Callahan and Mr. Carter were busy talking. Pretty soon Mike got restless. "Pop," he said, "can't we go outside and wait for you?"

"All right," said his father. "I'll be right along. You go sit in the car."

Mike and Peter walked back along the road and climbed into the car. But it was as hot as an oven inside.

"Let's go sit on the grass," said Peter. "It looks cool there."

So they climbed out and sprawled on the grass.

31

A faint breeze blew under the pine trees.

"It's nice here," said Peter.

"Uh-huh," said Mike. "What'll we do?"

He picked up a flat stone and skipped it across the water.

"Hey, are you supposed to throw things into the water?" Peter asked.

"No," said Mike. "But the stone is clean. It isn't like going swimming. Boy, I wish we could go swimming. We got gypped this morning."

"Why can't we swim in it?" Peter asked.

"How would you like it if people went swimming in your drinking water?" Mike retorted. "Come on, let's have a catch," and he pulled a baseball out of his pocket and tossed it to Peter.

Peter hurled it back. Mike picked up a stick and batted it. It went sailing out over the water.

"Oh, boy, now look!" said Mike. "And it's a new ball, too."

"What will your father say?" Peter asked.

"He'll be mad, I guess," said Mike. "Look, it's floating pretty near. Maybe I could get it."

He took off his shoes and waded out carefully. He reached out with the stick to coax the ball nearer.

"Hey, look out!" Peter called, and just then Mike slipped on something and sat down with a big splash. Then he was floundering about in the water with a scared look on his face.

"It's deep!" he gasped.

Suddenly Peter realized that Mike couldn't swim. In a flash he jumped up and plunged in. He grabbed Mike by the shirt and paddled to

33

shore. He dragged him up on the grass and stood there panting.

"Wow!" Mike breathed. "I was scared! Thanks a lot!"

"Why didn't you say you couldn't swim?" Peter demanded.

"I can swim in shallow water," said Mike. "But it got deep all of a sudden. Gosh! Pop will be mad!"

"Here he comes now," said Peter.

Mr. Carter was hurrying toward them. "Come on, now, you kids, we've got to step on it," he called, and then he caught sight of them, both dripping wet. "What happened?" he exclaimed.

"I—I fell in," Mike mumbled, staring at the ground, "and Peter saved me. I—I almost drowned."

"You fell in!" said his father, looking out at the baseball bobbing along on the water, and then looking back severely at his son.

"It's true," said Peter. "It gets deep all of a sudden right beyond the edge."

Mr. Carter nodded. "I know," he said. "And

Mike can't swim in deep water. I'm glad you were here, Peter. Mike, I'm ashamed of you. You know it's against the law to go swimming in the reservoir. I hope one of the Water Supply police doesn't come along. Would I be embarrassed! Well, get in the car and get some dry clothes out of the suitcases, both of you. I don't want you catching cold on top of everything else."

Peter wasn't worried about that. There was something else bothering him. "What will happen to the water?" he asked. "Will it be dirty now? And what about the baseball? Will it get into the pipes?"

"Don't let that worry you," said Mr. Carter, smiling. "There's a screen down there in the bottom to keep dirt from getting into the pipes. So even if the baseball got waterlogged and sank, it wouldn't go through. The water is all chlorinated, too, before it gets into the mains. I think there's enough chlorine to kill any germs you and Mike put in. Besides, look at that."

Mr. Carter pointed to a cluster of fountains not far from the road.

"Those are aerators," he said. "The sun and air kill germs and make the water taste good."

"A malted milk would taste good to me," said Mike.

"Mike," said his father sternly, "I ought to take you back and leave you in the reservoir."

"You can't, Pop," said Mike. "I fell in by accident, but it's against the law to *throw* anything in."

Now they were getting close to the city. Cars flashed by, more than Peter had ever seen. It was beginning to get dark. Solid blocks of buildings stood out black against the deep blue sky. Thousands of lighted windows and street lamps shone like diamonds. They were driving through city streets. People were sitting out on the stoops trying to cool off. Peter was almost asleep when Mr. Carter finally stopped the car and said, "Here we are."

PART III

Peter was so sleepy that night that he could hardly shake hands with Mike's mother. He ate his dinner and tumbled into bed. It was past nine o'clock when he woke up next morning. He was surprised to find himself in a strange room. It took him several minutes to remember that he wasn't at home, but visiting Mike in a city apartment.

"Hurry up," Mike called to him. "We're going downtown to meet Pop. He's gone to his office already."

Peter dressed and came to breakfast. Now that he had a good look at Mrs. Carter he saw that she had red hair like Mike's and that she looked like him when she smiled.

"It's a hot time for you to come to the city," she said. "And it's too bad you boys can't go for a swim. The pools are all closed on account of the water shortage."

Mike's face turned red. "I guess we don't want to go swimming anyhow," he said. "Not after yesterday. Pop said he'd take us to a movie. It will be cool there."

Mrs. Carter nodded. "I guess so," she said. "Though they may have to cut out air cooling. That takes water, too, you know."

Peter was puzzled. "I had a shower this morning," he said. "There's plenty of water, but everybody keeps talking about a shortage."

"Oh, we still have enough pressure," said Mrs. Carter. "It's just that we have to be careful. We don't want to use up so much water that we don't have pressure."

"But if everybody is careful, will you still need more reservoirs?"

Mrs. Carter smiled at him. "I know what you're thinking," she said. "This is an emergency, on account of the dry spell. But we still need a bigger water supply. Just wait till you see how big this city is. And it's getting bigger every day."

Peter looked out of the window at the miles of apartment houses. Some were small and some

were much taller than the one the Carters lived in. Some roofs had big tanks on legs.

"What are those for?" Peter asked.

"They're water tanks," said Mike.

"Is there one on this house?" said Peter.

"No," said Mike. "This is only six stories high, so the city pressure pushes the water up. But if a building is higher than that, it has to have pumps in the cellar. Then they pump water up to the tank on the roof so it can run down to the apartments."

"You certainly know a lot," said Peter.

Mike grinned. "You would, too, if you heard nothing but water, water, water every single day. Well, come on, let's get going."

Out in the street it was really hot. The sun beat down on the pavement, and the heat of the cement burned through Peter's shoes. Mike led the way to the subway. It was crowded with people.

"I didn't know there *were* so many people," said Peter.

The train rocked along through the tunnel and at every stop more people got on. When at last they got off and came up into the sunlight, the buildings reached up to the sky. Peter hurried after Mike. He didn't want to lose him in these crowded streets. He wondered how Mike could find his way. But Mike seemed to know just where he was going. He darted in and out among the people and led the way through the traffic. Peter couldn't help admiring him.

Suddenly there was a loud clanging. Fire engines came swooping down a side street.

"Come on!" yelled Mike. "Let's see the fire!"

He started to run and Peter sprinted after him. The firemen jumped off the truck and attached a hose to a hydrant. They ran into a building with the end of the hose. Soon they came out.

"False alarm," somebody said.

"Aw, shucks," said Mike. "I was hoping we'd see a good one."

"What would they do if one of those tall buildings caught fire?" Peter asked. "How would they get the water 'way up there?"

"Oh, they've got big pumping engines that shoot a stream of water ten stories high," said Mike. "Boy, that's something! And when the building is higher than that, there's an outlet on every floor for the firemen to connect their hoses."

"But suppose there wasn't enough water," said Peter. "I bet it takes a lot of water to get up that high."

"Yes," said Mike. "That's one thing they're afraid of. If the water gets too low, there won't be enough pressure to fight fires. Those big engines would empty the mains pretty quick. Pop says they use twelve thousand gallons a *minute!* Well, come on."

They walked along. Near a street corner a crowd of people were watching something that made a loud clattery noise. Two men were working with a big drill, cutting a hole in the road. The drill was attached to a gasoline engine that chugged noisily, and nearby was a green truck with the words "Department of Water Supply" on it.

"That's our truck!" Mike shouted in Peter's ear. "There must be a leak in there."

Peter peered into the hole. There was a maze of pipes down in the ground. Some were thin, some were middle-sized, and there was one big thick pipe more than three feet across.

"Wow! What's that big pipe?" Peter shouted.
"That's a water main," Mike yelled back.

"Come on!"

He hurried on, and Peter hurried after him.

"Hey, I didn't know water mains were that big," he panted.

"Oh, they aren't all that big," said Mike. "Some of them are smaller—you know, where there aren't so many big buildings. Here we are."

He led Peter through the door of a very tall building. A great many people were walking about on the polished marble floor. There were two rows of elevators. The boys got into one that was marked "Express." In a minute they were shooting upward.

They got off at the twenty-third floor, and Mike led the way into an office. There were men working at desks. They all knew Mike.

"Hello, there," said a gray-haired man sitting near a window. "Your father stepped out for a minute. He'll be back soon. Come on over and sit down."

But Peter didn't want to sit down. He stared out of the window at the city far below. There were miles and miles of buildings and parks and streets. There was a river, with bridges across it, and beyond that there were more buildings. Steam and smoke rose from chimneys. Washing hung from clotheslines. Eight million people lived here!

47

A voice behind him said, "Well, Peter, how do you like the city?"

It was Mr. Carter. Peter turned around and looked at him.

"It's—it's terrific!" he said. "I never thought it would be like this. What are those red buildings down there?"

"Factories," said Mr. Carter. "They're building more of them all the time. And more people are moving into the city. Now do you see why we need a lot of water?"

"Uh-huh," said Peter.

"Well, come on. We'll take a look at the office and then go out and have some lunch. This is the leak department. People phone in here when there's a leak and the men go and fix it."

"But how do they know where the leak is?" Peter asked.

"That's a good question," said Mr. Carter. "Sometimes they see water bubbling up in the street. But sometimes it seeps away through the ground. Then they don't know till the man at some gatehouse sees the pressure going down on

48

the gauges. Or sometimes people turn on a faucet and the water doesn't run out."

"And then what?" said Peter.

"The men go out and dig up the street," said Mr. Carter. "They turn off the water at the gatehouse, and they fix the pipe. When there's a shortage, the way there is now, they have to work fast. Look here."

He pointed to a case where there were pieces of broken pipe. There were signs on them: *50,000 gallons per day lost through this leak. 35,000 gallons lost through this defective tap.*

There were some pieces of wooden pipe. "This is the kind of pipe we used to have a hundred years ago," he said. "Imagine that!"

They went down in the elevator, and Mr. Carter took them to a big restaurant for lunch.

As they were finishing their dessert, Mike asked, "What are we going to do this afternoon, Pop?"

Mr. Carter frowned. "I'm sorry," he said. "I thought I would have the afternoon off to take you around. But there's a meeting I must go to. Do you think you can amuse yourselves?"

"Oh, sure," said Mike. "Just give us some money and we'll go to the movies. You can take us somewhere tomorrow."

The movie was a Western, full of action and hard riding. The boys sat on the edge of their seats and ate popcorn. When they came out into the street, they blinked at the daylight.

"That was a good picture," said Mike. "Action. That's what I like. Nothing exciting ever happens in real life."

"What do you mean, nothing exciting happens?" said Peter. He felt as if things had been happening for the last two days without stopping. Why, it was exciting just to walk around the streets and look at all the stores and the people.

But it was hot after being in the cool theater.

"I wish we could take a swim," said Mike. "How am I ever going to learn if I never get any practice?"

"We could go home and take a shower," said Peter. So they headed for home.

When they got there, Mrs. Carter was out. There was a plate of sandwiches on the table and a note saying she would be back at five.

"Let's take a shower first and eat later," said Mike. "You go first."

So Peter got into the tub and turned on the faucet. Only a thin trickle of water came out. He opened the faucet wider. A few more drops splashed on his bare stomach.

"Hey, Mike!" he called. "How do you work this shower?"

"Just turn the faucet," said Mike.

"But it doesn't run," said Peter. "Maybe I'm doing it wrong."

Mike came and looked. He fiddled with the

faucet. "Maybe the janitor is fixing something," he said. "They turn off the water when they work on the pipes."

"But then there wouldn't be *any* water," said Peter. "Now there's just a little."

"That's right," said Mike. "Well, maybe everybody in the house is using the water at once."

But Peter was thinking of something Mr. Carter had said. Sometimes people turned on a faucet and the water didn't run out.

"Maybe there's a leak," he said.

"Oh, boy! I bet that's right!" said Mike. "Come on; we'd better find the janitor."

"Wait till I get my clothes on," said Peter.

They raced down to the janitor's apartment and knocked. There was no answer. They looked for him in the yard and out in the street.

"Let's look in the furnace room," said Mike. He led Peter through a dark passageway into a still darker room. A big black shape stood in the middle. That was the furnace. Peter could hardly see a thing. He took a step—his feet were wet!

"Hey! There's water on the floor!" he shouted.

Now Mike found the light. There was a deep pool of water at one end of the cellar.

"We ought to turn the water off, I guess," he said. "I'm not quite sure where you do it, though."

"Well, in our house there's a valve near where the pipe comes into the cellar," said Peter. "Let's see. It ought to be around here somewhere." He waded into the water, shoes and all. He reached down and grabbed a handle. It spun round in his hands.

"Say, there's something the matter with the

valve," he said. "It's broken. We can't turn it off. And the water's coming in fast."

"We'd better phone the department," said Mike. "I guess they'll have to turn it off out in the street."

He raced up the stairs with Peter after him. He seized the telephone and dialed a number.

"Water Supply Department?" he said. "I want to report a leak. It's inside the cellar, but the valve is busted and we can't turn the water off. No, the janitor is out. Okay, we'll be looking for you." He gave the address and hung up.

The boys ran down to the street. In a few minutes a green truck arrived. The men jumped out and ran to the cellar. It wasn't long before they had the water turned off at the main so that it stopped coming in. Then they pumped the water out of the cellar.

By this time the neighbors had heard about it. They crowded into the basement. Somebody found the janitor.

"Kids!" he grumbled. "Always up to mischief."

One of the men turned and looked at him. "You ought to be glad there were a couple of kids here," he said. "They saved you a lot of trouble. Now you'd better hurry and get a plumber. It's inside the house, so we're not supposed to fix that valve."

The men got back into their truck and drove off, and the boys went up to change their wet clothes—just in time, too, for as they were squeezing the water out Mrs. Carter came home. But she didn't scold. She was very pleased with them.

"You boys thought fast and did the right thing," she said. "You make a good team."

Peter was surprised when he thought about that. Just a few days ago he wouldn't have cared what happened. But now he did care. He didn't want the water to be wasted or the cellar flooded, because these people were his friends.

That evening at supper Mike's father heard what the boys had done and he was pleased, too. "You two ought to get a reward for this," he said. "I ought to take you out tomorrow and give you a good time, but I won't be able to. They told me at the meeting today that I'll have to take another trip up to Peter's part of the country and I'll have to go tomorrow. But I'll be back in a few days and then we'll have some fun."

Suddenly Mike said, "Look! It's getting dark!"

The sky was covered with dark clouds. There was a growl of thunder, and lightning flashed.

"It's raining!" Mike yelled, jumping up and

running to the window. The big drops were coming down, splashing against the glass. Soon streams of water were running down the gutters into the sewers. It seemed a shame that all that water should be wasted.

"All it does is wash the streets," said Mr. Carter. "The rain won't do us much good unless it rains in the watershed."

"I hope it does," said Peter. But there was something that bothered him. It was true the Carters were his friends. And the city was big and exciting. But that wasn't enough reason for flooding his valley. There had to be more than that. He just had to know.

"Mr. Carter," he said, "there's something I'd like to ask you."

"Sure, Peter," said Mr. Carter.

"I still don't see why country people should

give up their homes for city people. I mean the city needs the water and all that, but what's the *real* reason?"

Mr. Carter nodded gravely. "There's a very important reason," he said. "Tell me, Peter, where does your father sell his milk and vegetables?"

"Well," said Peter, "I guess they go to the city, mostly."

"Then city people do something for you," said Mr. Carter. "They buy your vegetables."

"Sure," said Peter, "but what would they do if we didn't raise them?"

"They'd be out of luck," said Mr. Carter. "They need you to raise them."

"But you need us, too," Mike broke in. "The factories are in the city. That's where they make things for farms—machinery and stuff. And clothes. And—and everything."

"But we pay money for those things," said Peter. "I guess that helps the city people."

"It certainly does," said Mr. Carter. "But factories need water, and so do the people who work in them. So you've got to help us out with vegetables and money and water, too."

Peter nodded. For the first time it all really made sense.

"I guess we all sort of help each other," he said. "But I certainly wish I knew where we're going to live when you flood our valley." Suddenly he wanted to be back there. He wanted to talk to his father and find out what was going to happen to their home.

"I know what you could give us for a reward for finding the leak," he said. "Take us back with you when you go tomorrow, and let Mike visit us for a while. If he wants to, I mean."

Mike grinned at him. "You bet I do," he said.

PART IV

After breakfast the next morning they started. It had rained all night. Now the sun was shining again, but the air was cooler. The trees had been washed by the rain and everything looked fresh

59

and green. Mr. Carter turned on the car radio.

"We had an inch of rain in the watersheds last night," the announcer said. "It was the first hard rain in more than a month."

Peter felt good. He was glad it had rained. He was glad he had gone to the city, but it was nice getting back to the country. He could hardly wait to ask his father about the new farm.

They drove all day. Now it was evening, and they were driving along the creek road.

"Pretty soon we'll be there," said Peter, looking for the white house and the red barn. "Right around this bend."

And there was his house. But what was the matter with it? It was crooked. It was all turned around and it was up on some funny rollers!

Mr. Carter stopped the car, and Peter jumped out. Mother came out of the house and smiled at him.

"We're moving," she said.

"You mean the whole house?" Peter exclaimed. "The barn, too?"

"Everything," said Mother. "Even the calf shed."

Sure enough, the shed was up on rollers and the calf stuck its head out and bleated, "Ba-a-a!"

"Where are we moving to?" Peter demanded.

"It was going to be a surprise," Mother said. "But now you're home ahead of time, we'll have to tell you. Father bought a farm up at the head of the valley. I think you'll like it."

"When are we starting?" said Peter.

"First thing tomorrow morning," his mother said.

Right after breakfast next day men came with tractors. They attached ropes to the house and the moving began. It was certainly funny to see the house being pulled along the road, like an enormous trailer. It took a long time—more than a week. Every night when they sat down to supper they looked out at a different view.

At last the moving was over. The house was in its new place, settled on its new foundation.

The next morning, when the boys ran outdoors, Peter saw something he had never seen before. Instead of looking up at the blue hills, he was looking down at them. At his feet was the valley, which one day would be a great blue lake, and on the other side was the sunrise!

"I like this place," said Peter. "I'm glad we came."

EVERYDAY ADVENTURE STORIES

Grades 1–2
THE THREE J'S
How a family works and plays together.

Grades 2–3
BROWNIE MAKES THE HEADLINES
Step by step information about how a newspaper is made.

CROSS-COUNTRY BUS RIDE
Excellent picture of bus travel, road and camping problems.

TIM AND THE BRASS BUTTONS
About policemen and the rules of safety.

Grades 2–4
MILKMAN FREDDY
Life on a dairy farm.

WIRES UP!
About communications, and a family hobby, bird watching.

Grades 3–4
PEANUT BUTTER MASCOT
About the many uses of peanuts.

PIERRE COMES TO P.S. 20
Everyone has something to contribute to the American way of life.

TOMMY AND THE ORANGE-LEMON TREE
About the citrus fruit industry.

Grades 3–5
CHRISTMAS-TREE SAM
How Christmas trees are grown and marketed.

COAST GUARD TO THE RESCUE
The exciting work of the Coast Guard.

FIREMAN FOR A DAY
About firefighting and a dramatic rescue.

FISHERMAN JODY
Bringing fish to the Fulton Fish Market.

JERRY'S TREASURE HUNT
About the Department of Sanitation.

KRISTA AND THE FROSTY PACKAGES
Information about frozen foods.

MAKE WAY FOR WATER
Tells how a big city is supplied with water.

MERRILY WE ROLL ALONG
Trucks, trucking and highway control.

SARA'S LUCKY HARVEST
About one of our most important crops—potatoes.

A TUGBOAT TOOTS FOR TERRY
The work of the New York harbor tugboats.

6494